my HERO

words & pictures by

BRIAN BIGGS

Dial Books for Young Readers

LOOK! THERE!

A frightened feline!
CAUGHT in the CLUTCHES
of that TERRIBLE TREE!

DESPERATE to ESCAPE, is there any HOPE for HARRY? WHO will come forth and SAVE THE DAY?

She's QUICKER than LIGHTNING!
She's STRONGER than STEEL!
Disguised as an
ORDINARY KID,
she FLIES in the
FACE of DANGER!

WHO is this
MYSTERY MARVEL?
This DARING DEFENDER?
THiS GALLANT GiRL of
GREATNESS?!

"I'm Awesome Girl!

"I can turn invisible, I'm empowered with super-strength, I have amazing fighting skills..."

Abigail occasionally had to remind her father of her true nature as a defender of freedom and justice.

Abigail's father occasionally had to remind her to get off the toilet.

"You could slip and fall."

"Daddy! I can jump over tall buildings
and I can fly, you know."

"Okay, just stay where I can see you."

"I can run faster than *anybody*."

"All right, but watch where
you're going."

"You're not listening!
Do you remember when
I saved everyone from
the robot invasion?"

"Of course I remember,"
her father replied.

"I just don't want you to get hurt."

"I know you don't believe me, Daddy, but it's true.
If you ever get into trouble, I'll save you.
I'll be your hero."

"I know, Abigail," her father said as he went to make dinner.

"You'll always be my little hero."

"*Little hero?*

"That's *not* what I meant."

BUT THEN...

DOINK

YES, it's **AWESOME GIRL !**
Normally disguised as **ABIGAIL,** an ordinary little kid, **AWESOME GIRL** arrives to **SAVE** the **DAY !**

Let go of my Daddy !

No!

WHAC

HAHAHA

PURPLE OCTOPUS! Release the child's **FATHER!**

Why should I ? He never even LISTENS!

Well, he doesn't!

Once again, AWESOME GIRL, champion of the WORLD, SAVES THE DAY!!
AWESOME GIRL!
AWESOME GIRL!
AWESOME GIRL!
Awesome Girl!

And with the defeat of **PURPLE OCTOPUS**, **AWESOME GIRL** returns to **ORDINARY LIFE** just in time for dinner.

THE
END

for ROXANE and RYLiE
and KATE and EiLEY,
and especially TRAVIS.

Dial Books for Young Readers
An imprint of Penguin Random House LLC, New York

First published in the United States of America by Dial Books for Young Readers, an imprint of Penguin Random House LLC, 2022

Copyright © 2022 by Brian Biggs

Visit us online at penguinrandomhouse.com

Library of Congress Cataloging-in-Publication Data is available.

Manufactured in Spain
ISBN 9780525553380

2 4 6 8 10 9 7 5 3 1
EST

Design by Jennifer Kelly
Text handlettered by Brian Biggs

The illustrations in this book were created with inks, gouache, colored pencils, regular pencils, pastels, small bits of paper and glue, and the blood, sweat, and tears of raising my two kids into the heroes they've become.